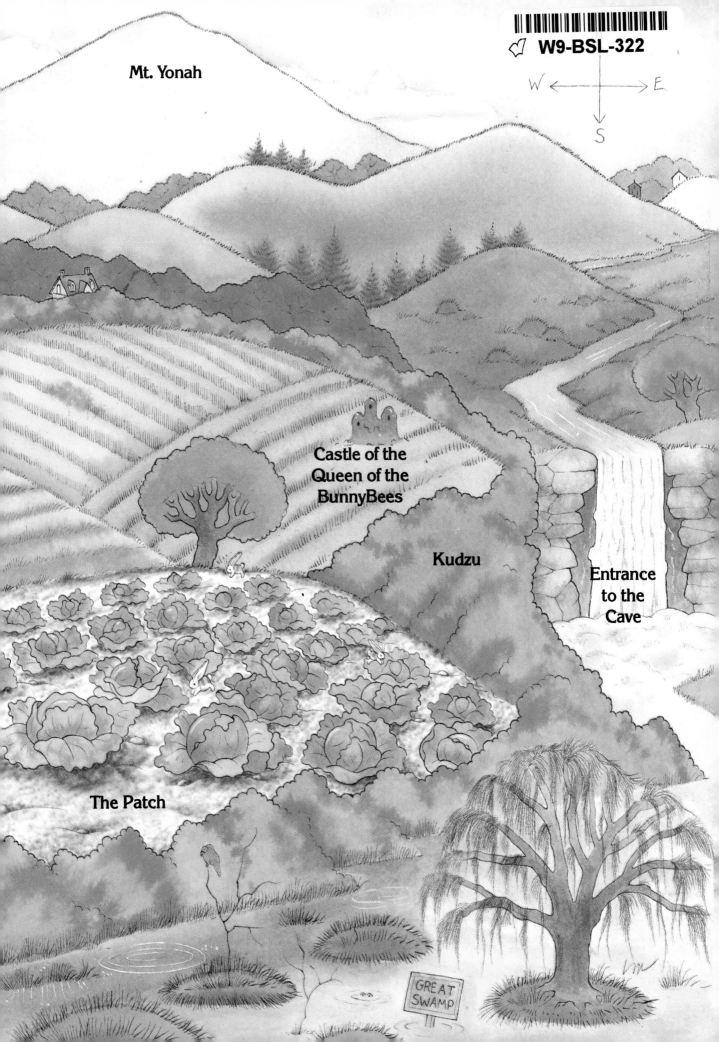

Library of Congress Cataloging in Publication Data: Callen, Larry. The just-right family. (Cabbage Patch kids). SUMMARY: Laura Sue finally finds just the right family to adopt her.
[1. Adoption—Fiction. 2. Family life—Fiction] I. Gailen, Judy, ill. II. Title. III. Series.
PZ7.C134Ju 1984 [E] 83-26263 ISBN 0-910313-26-1
Manufactured in the United States of America 1 2 3 4 5 6 7 8 9 0

The Just-Right Family

Story by Larry Callen
Pictures by Judy Gailen

Sometimes Laura Sue was happy and sometimes Laura
Sue was sad. Sometimes she was even happy-sad.
   She was happy when she was swimming,
   Or singing in the choir,
   Or collecting bugs, which was her favorite thing to do.

She was sad when she stubbed her toe,

Or had nothing to do on a rainy day,

Or when it was her turn to mop the floor, which was her most unfavorite thing to do.

She was happy-sad on adoption day, which was any day when one of the Cabbage Patch Kids went off to live with a new family.

"Why do you feel happy-sad on adoption day?" asked her best friend, Beth Marie.

"When I see one of the other 'Kids get adopted, I feel all happy inside," said Laura Sue. "But at the same time I get a powerful sad feeling in my stomach. And I wonder if anyone will ever adopt me."

"Don't be sad, Laura Sue," said Beth Marie, trying to cheer up her friend. "You'll be adopted someday soon. I just know it. You are kind and thoughtful. You know lots of great jokes and you know more about bugs than anybody."

"Don't forget what Colonel Casey told us. There is a family waiting for every Cabbage Patch Kid. It just takes time for the right family to find the right 'Kid.'"

Laura Sue nodded, but she wasn't sure that she believed what her friend had said. She remembered the last time she had met a family, and she shuddered. It was one of the worst days of her life.

That day Colonel Casey took her through the underground tunnel to Babyland General Hospital. As soon as she walked in, Laura Sue began to get nervous. The very air in the room seemed to be pressing down on her body. She knew that if she wasn't careful, she was bound to do or say something wrong.

In the corner of the room sat a thin, pale woman. A stumpy little man with ears like cauliflowers stood next to her. They smiled at Laura Sue. They seemed kind, but Laura Sue didn't know what to say. She wanted to be adopted so powerful bad.

The thin woman nodded a greeting. "My dear, you are so very quiet. Tell Mr. Sneet and me something about yourself. What interests you?"

Laura Sue felt a little better. She had brought something with her that she knew would interest anyone who wanted to adopt her. She reached into the big pocket of her sweater.

"Yes, ma'm. Look at this."

She held out a large jar that she had made into an ant farm. The ants scurried about in the jar.

"Isn't it a dilly?" asked Laura Sue.

The thin woman turned a shade paler and moved back.

"It certainly is! But *please* put it away. I itch just looking at those crawly things."

Laura Sue hugged the ant farm to her and scrunched up her face feeling more miserable now than before. She started to shove the ant farm into her pocket, but her fingers fumbled, and the jar slipped from her hand. It bounced on the floor and shattered into a hundred pieces. Ants scooted every which way. Mrs. Sneet shrieked and rushed out of the room. It was the last time Laura Sue saw her.

She knew that the Sneets were not the right family for her, but Laura Sue couldn't help but feel kindly upset at what had happened. Soon, however, she had different feelings. Beth Marie came running up to her, a big grin on her face.

"Guess what? I am the happiest girl in the world! Colonel Casey said that tomorrow evening I'm fixin' to be adopted by the Mellowbys. They're a special kind of farmers, and really wonderful people. Can you guess what they raise?"

"Cows?" Laura Sue guessed. "Apples?"

"Wrong!" laughed Beth Marie. From behind her back she pulled a big catfish and held it up.

"Catfish farmers?" Laura Sue asked. She stared at the catfish. The catfish stared back.

"They raise them in ponds and sell them to the fish store. They eat some, too, but I'm sure that they eat other things as well."

Laura Sue wrinkled her nose. How could anyone eat catfish even once? Why, they had whiskers! Although she was feeling happy-sad about the news of Beth Marie's adoption, she certainly was glad she was not going to live on a catfish farm.

Laura Sue and Beth Marie spent their last night in the Cabbage Patch together telling stories and making plans to go on one last picnic in the morning.

"You are truly my best friend," said Beth Marie.

"And you are mine," said Laura Sue.

In the morning they got up nice and early.

"Time to get a wiggle on," said Beth Marie. "We want to have a heap o' fun today before I leave."

Laura Sue agreed. "But we'll have to be quiet. Colonel Casey wouldn't like us going alone," she said thinking about Lavendar McDade's gold mine and the sneaky Beau Weasel and Cabbage Jack who helped kidnap 'Kids to work the mine.

"I reckon we'll have to be a mite careful," said Beth Marie.

"But let's not worry about those two pests who work for Lavendar McDade," said Laura Sue. "We don't want anything to spoil our last day together."

The two girls started off when the dew was still sparkling on the grass. They soon left the Cabbage Patch behind. Laura Sue held Beth Marie's hand as they walked up a steep hill and into a meadow filled with wildflowers.

"We've come a far piece, and I'm plum wore out. Let's sit a spell," said Laura Sue.

They were resting on a log when they heard a snarling and hissing behind them.

"Oh no! It's Beau Weasel!" cried Laura Sue. "Maybe we can slow him down. Help me tie this jump rope across the path. I reckon he won't see it until it's too late, and it will trip him up as we get away."

The fierce snarling grew louder. Beth Marie was so scared that she dropped her end of the rope twice.

"Hurry!" cried Laura Sue. Finally the jump rope was stretched tight across the path. The girls got up and began to run.

"This way," said Beth Marie. "I think the river is over there. Beau Weasel hates water worse than a dog hates fleas. If we can make it to the river, we'll be safe."

"You can't fool me that easy," snarled Beau Weasel as he appeared at the edge of the clearing. He leaped over their rope and drew nearer to the frightened girls.

The girls ran.
The weasel came closer.
And closer.
"What'll we do now?" panted Beth Marie.

"Hold your nose and jump in," Laura Sue yelled.

They leaped into the water. The swift current pulled them under and carried them along, bouncing and swirling. Just when Laura Sue thought that her lungs were going to burst, she popped up to the surface like a cork. She gasped and took a deep breath.

The two girls floated downstream rapidly, twisting and turning in the rough water. Suddenly they came to a small ledge. They toppled over, and swoosh! Before they knew what was happening they were washed ashore.

They lay on the river bank panting.

"Are we safe?" asked Beth Marie.

"I reckon so, but I'm afraid that our picnic is ruined," Laura Sue answered with a weak smile.

The two sopping wet 'Kids quickly made their way back to the Cabbage Patch and told the others what had happened. A special guard was posted. Then Beth Marie packed, said happy-sad goodbyes to everyone, and climbed on Colonel Casey's back for her trip to her new family.

Without Beth Marie, life in the Cabbage Patch was lonely for Laura Sue.

Then one day the old stork brought Laura Sue a letter from Beth Marie. It read:

Dear Laura Sue:

I love it here. The Mellowbys are wonderful to me. We live in a nice house, and have four horses, and right near the pasture are peach trees, loaded with the yummiest peaches you've ever tasted.

I can tell that I am going to live a happy life here. I hope some day you can come for a visit.

Your friend,
Beth Marie

"Oh, I wish I could go and visit Beth Marie," thought Laura Sue. "The Mellowbys's farm sounds so wonderful." And secretly Laura Sue wished the Mellowbys had adopted her too. Even if she had to eat catfish every day. "But they already have Beth Marie," she sighed. "And besides, who'd want a 'Kid like me who likes bugs?"

Laura Sue was beginning to feel sorry for herself when she heard Colonel Casey's blustery voice calling the 'Kids to meet him at Babyland General for a special announcement. They all gathered by the flag pole, sitting cross-legged on the grass. Laura Sue sat at the very back, still feeling more sad than happy, remembering how she and Beth Marie had sometimes gotten Colonel Casey's dander up with their giggling and talking at such gatherings.

Laura Sue looked up at Colonel Casey wondering what the announcement would be.

Suddenly, the Mellowbys and Beth Marie walked up front and stood next to the Colonel. Beth Marie's eyes searched the crowd and found Laura Sue in the last row. Laura Sue was

surprised to see her friend, and waved happily. Then Beth Marie leaned over and whispered something to one of the 'Kids in the front row. That 'Kid turned and whispered into the ear of the one next to him.

"Silence, please," said Colonel Casey. "Now, as you can see, our good friends, the Mellowbys, are here."

But Laura Sue was barely listening to the old stork. Her eyes followed the whispering. What was the message? By now it had moved all the way across the front row of seats, then, snakelike, started across the second row.

"These fine folks say that if having one Cabbage Patch Kid around the house is so much fun they imagine it'd be twice as nice having two."

The whispered message had snaked its way to the row directly in front of her when Laura Sue realized that Colonel Casey had said something important. But she had only dimly heard his words.

"...a sister. That means bad luck for all you boys. But there will be other times..."

The whispered message was now coming to her row. It moved closer. It moved all the way to Jasper Bo, who sat right next to her. And then it stopped.

She waited. She looked at Jasper Bo. She elbowed him in the ribs. He grunted, but he didn't say a word. Why did he have to be such a tease? Angrily, she turned her attention to Colonel Casey.

"Will those sitting on the back row who believe the Mellowbys would be just the right family for them come on up here by me?" said Colonel Casey.

Laura Sue knew such wonderful wishes were never granted. It was a waste of time for her to go up there. But she went anyway, just to be near Beth Marie. She stood, her back to the seated 'Kids.

"Now, the second row?"

"The first?"

Laura Sue wondered how many Cabbage Patch Kids were standing behind her. The Mellowbys were going to have a hard time picking one 'Kid out of all those who wanted to go with them. She wished every one of them the best of luck. It would be nice if she could be the one.

"All right, now," said Colonel Casey. "This is going to be a mite easier than we thought…"

He spread a wing and pulled Laura Sue closer, "…since you are the only one standing."

Laura Sue turned quickly. Row after row of faces smiled at her. Not a single Cabbage Patch Kid had come forward. The other 'Kids had given her a very special present.

Beth Marie rushed over and took her hand.

"I whispered to the other 'Kids I wanted you," she said. "And I asked them to pass the word."

"We choose you to be Beth Marie's sister," said the Mellowbys. Each leaned over and kissed a cheek.

Laura Sue was glad that this time she didn't have an ant farm in her hand that could drop and break. She was also glad she didn't have a catfish staring her in the eye.

What she had was a new mother and father and sister. It was a happy time.

"Laura Sue," said Beth Marie, "do you think we could ride down the river again some time when nobody's chasing us?"

Laura Sue wiped a tear away and smiled. It was the very beginning of many happy times.

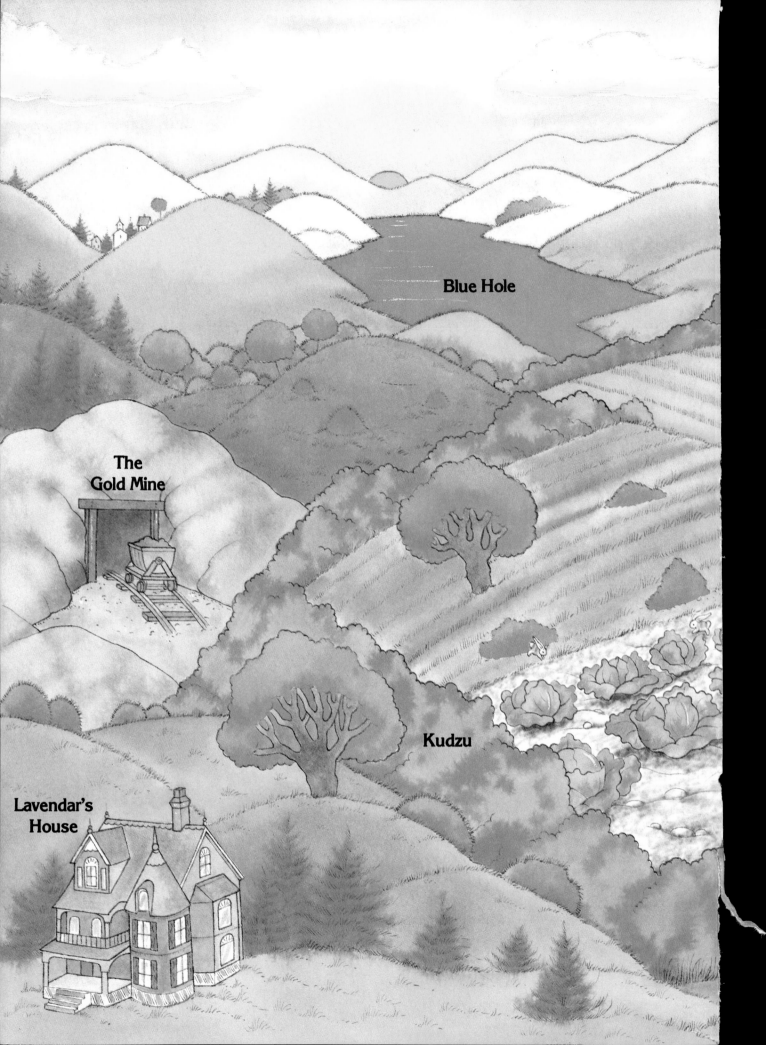

Blue Hole

The
Gold Mine

Kudzu

Lavendar's
House